Sooshewan
CHILD OF THE BEOTHUK

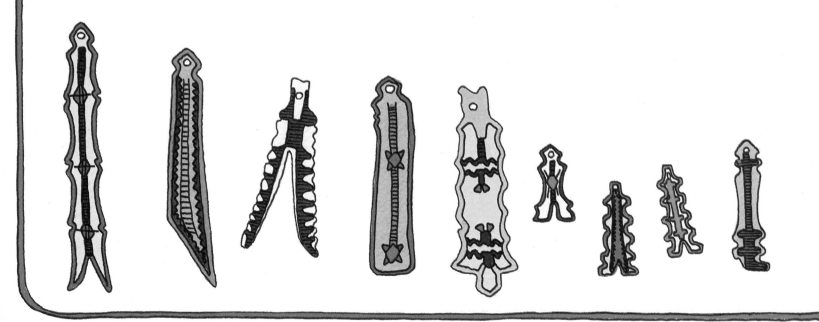

Sooshewan
CHILD OF THE BEOTHUK

by Donald Gale   illustrated by Shawn Steffler

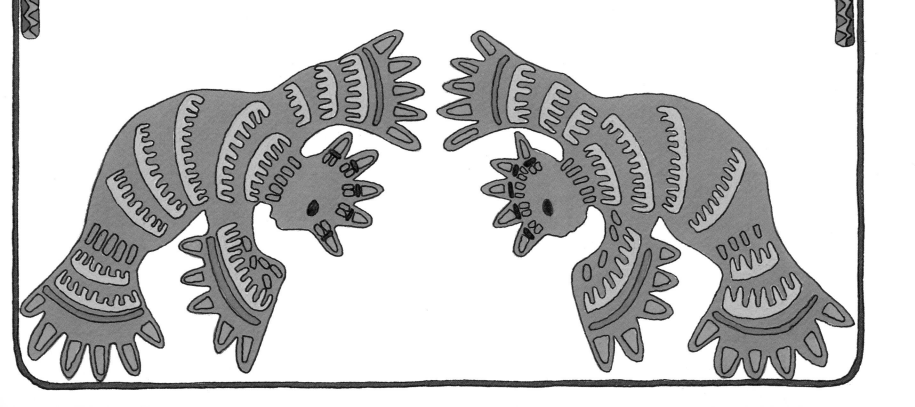

Canadian Cataloguing in Publication Data

Gale, Donald

   Sooshewan : child of the Beothuk

   ISBN 0-920911-15-3

1. Beothuk Indians — Juvenile fiction. 2. Indians of North America — Newfoundland — Juvenile fiction. I. Steffler, Shawn, 1950-. II. Title.

PS8563.A43S66 1988   jC813'.54   C88-098603 4
PZ7.G34So 1988

Breakwater gratefully acknowledges the financial support of The Canada Council which has helped make this publication possible.

The Publisher acknowledges the financial contribution of the Cultural Affairs Division of the Department of Culture, Recreation and Youth, Government of Newfoundland and Labrador, which has helped make this publication possible.

for
Paula, Susan,
Clara and David

Sooshewan was a Beothuk girl. She lived in a mamateek at the edge of a lake with her mother and father, three younger brothers, her grandmother, her uncle and two cousins, older girls.

The winter had been long and cold. This was the month when the ice should be melting and the people should be going down the river to the sea to hunt seals and sea birds. But Gidgeathuc, the wind, still blew his icy breath every day and the snow was too deep for travelling. The ice on the lake was so thick that they could not fish. Everyone was hungry.

Sooshewan woke early and snuggled close to her mother. She could hear her father, Monathook, moving around the mamateek, taking his bow and arrows and harpoon down from their hanging places.

"Where are you going, Father?" whispered Sooshewan.

"Hunting," replied her father. "I will return soon and you can tell everyone that I will have meat."

"Bring a bidesook," said the girl. She had not tasted fresh seal meat for many months and the thought of it increased her hunger.

As her father pushed through the caribou-skin door, Sooshewan felt cold air on her face. She heard her grandmother cough. She knew Grandmother was sick and needed good food. The caribou meat and fish were gone. Of all they had put away for winter, there remained only a small bag of powdered eggs mixed with fat.

By the time it was full daylight, the family was up. Sooshewan's mother spooned the egg mixture into the children's bowls, making the same joke she always made.

"Here is some salmon. Have a little slice of caribou tongue. Some fat blueberries for the baby. Don't eat too much, everyone."

Today she added, "Save room for the seal Monathook will bring."

She took only a small portion for herself. Sooshewan knew that the older people ate almost nothing to leave more for the children.

Grandmother did not get up. Sooshewan offered the old woman some of her food but she turned her head away. For a moment, Sooshewan was glad that she would not have to share her food. Immediately she was ashamed of her thought and left the mamateek.

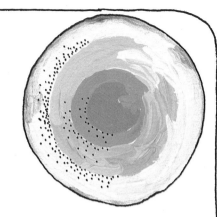

It had snowed during the night and outside everything was white: the four mamateeks that made up their winter village, the trees, the lake. Yesterday's tracks were covered. The sun was pale but there was no wind and it was not nearly as cold as it had been for a long time.

Sooshewan followed her uncle as he visited each of the large families in the other mamateeks, telling everyone that Monathook had gone to hunt. He spoke with Ossanweemet, the oldest man of the village.

"Monathook is the best hunter," said Ossanweemet. "He knows where the seals can be found. He may have gone south to look for early returning caribou."

Ossanweemet was a little worried about the weather. "Washewiush, the moon, had circles around her last night. This might bring snow and wind. Not even Monathook can hunt in a snowstorm."

Sooshewan spent the rest of the day helping repair the birchbark canoes that would take people down the river when the ice broke up. The men examined each canoe and decided which pieces of bark had to be replaced. Sooshewan sharpened bone awls on a rock. Her mother used split spruce roots to sew strips of bark in place on the light wooden frames. As Sooshewan watched her mother make the holes and push the roots through, forming perfect, neat stitches, she wished she could have a turn doing grown-up work.

"Sooshewan, my little woaseesk, do not wish to be grown up too quickly. You will have hard work to do soon enough."

Sooshewan did not like to be called *woaseesk*, little girl. Her mother thought of her as a little girl and did not seem to notice that she was almost a *woas-sut*, woman.

In the late afternoon, Sooshewan heard a shout. She ran to the edge of the clearing and saw one of the older boys returning to the village, waving something in the air. Proudly, he showed her three ptarmigan he had killed.

The birds were cleaned and put into a birchbark pot of water. The women added hot rocks to the pot until the birds were cooked. Nearly everyone in the village crowded around as the young hunter ladled out the hot soup.

Sooshewan squatted on her heels, anxious to enjoy her meal. But suddenly she got up and hurried to her mamateek.

"Grandmother," she called as she entered. "Wake up. I've brought you some soup."

The old woman only coughed. Sooshewan knelt and put her arm under Grandmother's shoulders and helped her sit up. She was surprised at how little her grandmother weighed. It seemed she might break like dry twigs.

As Sooshewan fed her grandmother the broth, she thought how much like a baby this old, old person was— small, soft and helpless. In the near darkness of the mamateek, Sooshewan forgot her hunger and gently rocked her grandmother.

After a while, she laid the old woman down in her sleeping place and smoothed the long grey hair and blanket.

Grandmother whispered, "Thank you, woaseesk," and squeezed her granddaughter's hand.

"I am Sooshewan, Grandmother."

Grandmother's eyes flashed for a moment as she looked at Sooshewan.

"You are growing up, Sooshewan," Grandmother said. "You are no longer a little girl. I am old and will die soon, perhaps even before the sun warms the earth again."

The old woman breathed deeply and then continued. "When I was young, I was frightened of death but now I welcome it. I have talked with the dead. They are waiting for me. Do not cry for me after I am gone, but give yourself to your people who are living."

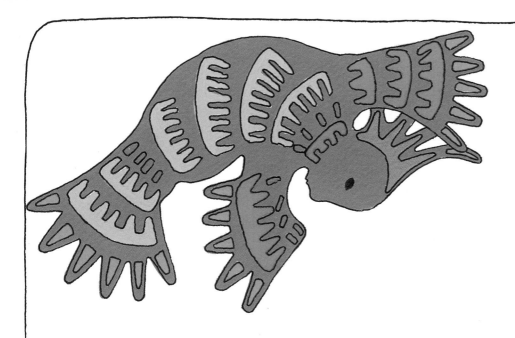

The old woman seemed to go to sleep then and Sooshewan went to eat. But the food was gone and she took her hunger to bed.

Sooshewan lay awake for a long time. It was the warmest night since winter had come. Above the sleeping sounds she could hear the drip of melting snow. The sound made her think of summer when food would be plentiful. Her hungry body longed for pink trout and salmon, fat seal meat, mussels from the sea bed, juicy raspberries. She hoped her father had been lucky. Imagining the greasy, laughing faces of her people gathered around a pot of seal meat, Sooshewan fell asleep.

"Sooshewan...Sooshewan," came a rattling whisper, arousing the girl out of a dream of silver salmon in sunny pools.

"Sooshewan..."

"Yes, Grandmother. What do you want?"

"Your father needs help."

"What do you mean, Grandmother? Where is he?"

"He is far to the north by the sea. Someone must go to him."

Sooshewan leaned over her grandmother and shook her gently, pleading, "Please tell me what's happened to him. Where is he?"

But the old woman spoke no more.

"Oh, Grandmother! Mother, wake up!" Sooshewan cried.

Soon everyone was up, trying to calm Sooshewan. Uncle lit a fire. Sooshewan's mother realized how sick Grandmother was and made root medicine for her. But she was in a deep sleep and would not take any.

Sooshewan begged her uncle to go and find her father.

"My child," he said, "I cannot go now. It is dark and the wind is blowing." He went to the doorway. "Snow has fallen. Your father's tracks are covered."

"But he needs help. Something has happened to him," Sooshewan pleaded.

"Sooshewan, go to sleep," said her uncle. "Do not let the dreams of an old woman frighten you. Your father has spent many winter nights away from home. He has made a comfortable shelter of boughs."

Sooshewan, hungry and fearful, spent the night in troubled dreams of running from something, and drowning, and all the terrible things that haunt people in their worst nights.

Grandmother died quietly in the night.

In the morning the whole village helped to prepare her funeral. The women dressed her in a robe of fur-trimmed deerskin with rows of shells and beads around the bottom. They put new moccasins on her feet. They made a cocoon of birchbark around her and covered the bark with red ochre. The men built a high platform in a clearing not far from the village.

The old woman would be placed on the platform and covered with branches. In the spring she would be buried in a grave with her things: her combs, her bowl, and the strings of shell beads she had made with the great patience of old age. In the spring there would be food to place in her grave and Monathook, her son, would perform the ceremony of sending away the dead.

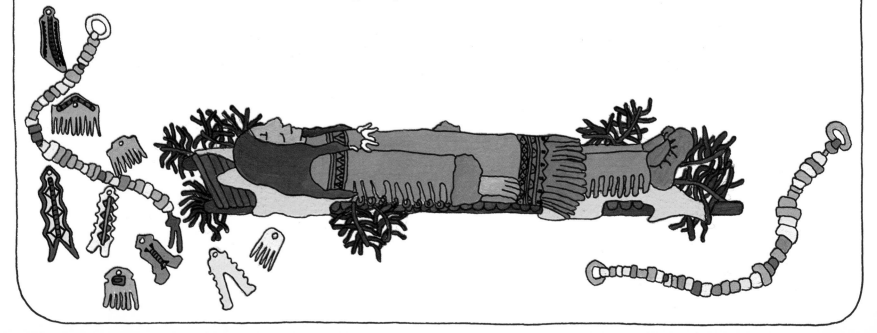

As the preparations were being made, Sooshewan and her mother spoke about Grandmother's warning.

"I believe you, Sooshewan," her mother said. "But there is nothing I can do. Most of the men are too sick or weak from hunger to travel now in the deep snow and unsettled weather. If we lose our hunters, there will be no one to get food when things are better.

"The men say it would be impossible to find your father's tracks now that the snow has covered them. They say Monathook can take care of himself in any situation."

"But Grandmother said Father needs help. Someone must go," pleaded Sooshewan.

"Some of the men don't believe there is reason to go. They say your grandmother's spirit would have spoken to an elder, not a child, in real danger. They say an empty stomach can bring bad dreams."

"I'm not a child and I did not dream this, Mother," Sooshewan said.

"I know," said her mother. "But we must both believe that if the old woman saw your father in trouble, her spirit will find a way to help him."

All the people gathered to accompany the old woman's body to its resting place. Sooshewan watched the men lift her grandmother on a stretcher of poles and deerskin. They followed old Ossanweemet as he walked slowly, chanting a spirit song.

Some were crying, but Sooshewan did not weep for her grandmother. She remembered the old woman's words about death. She also remembered the message about her father. As her people moved off into the woods, Sooshewan knew what she must do.

She made sure no one was looking and ducked out of sight behind a tree. As soon as everyone had gone, she went to her mamateek. Into a deerskin bag she packed a pair of moccasins, two iron pyrite fire stones, a small pouch of down, a stone axe and a knife. She took a small throwing stick, her snowshoes and fur mittens and left the mamateek. Once outside, she tied on her snowshoes, hoisted her bundle over her shoulder and headed north.

It was not yet midday and the sun was shining. Sooshewan knew that she could go north by keeping the sun at her back. She also knew that the river which ran from their lake flowed north to the sea, but turned and twisted on its way. Sooshewan was in too much of a hurry to follow the river.

There were no trails and Sooshewan constantly had to make detours to find open space for travelling. The heavy snow stuck to her snowshoes and she had to stop often to shake it off. In her caribou coat and leggings, she soon became hot.

Sooshewan walked until the sun was low, farther than she had ever walked before. She was so tired and hungry that her head felt light and she knew she was staggering.

Sooshewan stopped for a moment to rest. In front of her was a stand of tall spruce trees, their down-swept, snow-laden branches touching the ground, forming natural shelters. They looked so inviting that she stumbled toward them. Then she noticed movement in the trees. Perched on their branches was a number of ptarmigan.

She eased her throwing stick down in her hand until she held it near one end. Slowly, she crept closer until she was within striking distance. The birds had not stopped their murmuring and soft clucking. She brought her stick crashing down on the nearest bird. Immediately the others flew up in noisy confusion and flapped off over the tree tops. The wounded bird thrashed about, squawking desperately and staining the snow with blood. Sooshewan killed it quickly with a blow to the head.

Using bits of the down she had brought, dry twigs, and her fire stones, Sooshewan made a fire. She cleaned and plucked the bird and placed it on a stick over the fire. When she saw that the outside was browned, she could wait no longer and she ate the bird. The meat was nearly raw but never had anything tasted as good.

Refreshed, Sooshewan began walking again, following a barren ridge northwards. When darkness came, she dug a small cave in a wall of snow, curled up inside on a bed of green branches and fell asleep.

Light woke Sooshewan. From where she lay, she could see the moon, large and yellow resting on its edge between two tall fir trees.

She spoke out loud. "Grandmother, you have driven away the clouds so Washewiush can send down her light and I can see my way. Now help me find the shawwayet of the north."

After a quick scan of the sky, Sooshewan found what she was looking for, the north star. It told her which way to go. She walked until the moon went down and she could no longer see. Then, curled up in a cave in the snow, she slept until morning.

All the next day, Sooshewan followed the river. The weather was still mild but there was no sun.

Late that evening Sooshewan came to the sea. She was more tired and hungry than she had ever been in her life, too tired even to dig a hole in the snow. She fell into a deep sleep on the shore, listening to the familiar sounds of little waves and rolling gravel.

Sooshewan woke in daylight, under a layer of wet snow. The shore was covered in slabs of thick ice but the sea ice had moved off, driven by the southerly winds of the past few days. The tide was out and there was a wide strip of sandy gravel between the shore ice and the water. Sooshewan knew that in times like this when the moon was full, the sea retreated far from its shores and, if there were mussels, she could get them now.

Sooshewan walked stiffly over the rafted ice. She had not gone far when she came upon the first cluster of blue mussels. She tore them from the rocks. In a short while, she had a load of shellfish, seaweed and small stones that she could hardly carry.

Sooshewan went back to where her things were and dumped the load on the snow. She made a fire. Having no cooking pot to put them in, she tore the mussels loose and placed them around her fire. As each shell opened, she hooked the mussel away from the fire, allowed it to cool a little and ate it.

"Thank you, Grandmother," Sooshewan said. "My belly is full and I have some food left over. Please lead me to my father now."

Sooshewan gathered her things. Then she stood uncertainly in the thickly falling snow. To her left was the river mouth and beyond that a rocky coast with steep cliffs. To her right the shore was sandy. Last summer her family had camped near there. Which way should she go?

She pretended to be a hunter. Where would one find the mother seals and their pups? She saw no movement when she scanned the ice. But suddenly she remembered that there were small islands off to her left where whelping seals sometimes gathered.

Sooshewan crossed the river and walked easily on the bare, rocky beach, making good time. But the rough stones soon wore holes in the moccasins she was wearing. She threw them away and put on her other pair. After that, she walked on the ice. It was slippery and slowed her down but she could not risk wearing out these moccasins.

It was midday when Sooshewan rounded a point and saw the islands. But she also saw that she could no longer walk on the shore. The tide had risen and the sea lapped the bottom of the sheer cliff.

"Where do I go, Grandmother?" Sooshewan called.

But her voice seemed to get lost in the snow. Sooshewan knew her grandmother's spirit was not with her. She had come to the wrong place.

Tired and uncertain, she retraced her steps, stopping every few minutes to listen and look around. But she saw and heard nothing. She felt alone and hopeless and began to cry.

"Grandmother," she sobbed, "the daylight will soon be gone and I am lost. Maybe I will starve, or freeze, or a white bear from the north will kill me."

She felt sick and empty. The men must have been right. The message meant nothing. It was just the raving of a sick old woman or the dream of a hungry child.

"How could I save my father," thought Sooshewan. "I can't even take care of myself."

"Selfish girl," Sooshewan said, "thinking of myself when my father needs help."

She wiped away her tears and began to climb a narrow gully which cut into the cliff.

As she reached the top of the cliff, Sooshewan noticed a line of shadowed depressions near the trees. When she got closer, she saw that they were deep tracks covered by new snow. She followed them, running as fast as she could.

The tracks led to a rough bough shelter in the woods and Sooshewan knew that she had found her father. She hesitated, suddenly afraid of finding him dead. There was no sound except for her own breathing.

"Father! Father!" she called.

She peered into the shelter. Her father lay on a bed of fir boughs, wrapped in caribou skin. He was breathing but he did not seem to hear her. His face was hot and his lips were dry and cracked. Sooshewan pulled back the caribou skin. One foot was twisted; his ankle was broken.

Carefully she removed his moccasin and legging. He had a badly infected cut. Sooshewan began to care for her father as she had seen her mother care for her younger brothers. She bathed his forehead with snow and moistened his lips. There was a little birchbark and firewood in the shelter and she built a fire near the entrance. Quickly she folded birchbark to make a pail. Then she melted snow to bathe the wound.

She left the shelter to look for straight sticks to splint her father's ankle, balsam to seal the wound, and firewood. As she walked, she spoke to her grandmother.

"You have stayed with me and helped me find my father, Grandmother. Thank you. Now please help me take care of him."

When Sooshewan returned, she tore her deerskin bag into strips and used them to tie the splints in place on her father's leg. She put balsam on the wound before she wrapped it.

Through the night, she worked to keep the fire going and fight her father's fever. Toward morning, he seemed a little better and Sooshewan, unable to fight sleep any longer, dozed off.

Though she did not sleep long, it was fully light when she woke. She fought her tiredness. She knew her father needed food. She remembered her mussels. She could eat some and make a broth for her father. She stumbled out of the shelter to get more firewood, only dimly aware of what she was doing.

As she fed her father the broth, she realized he was better. His fever did not burn so and his breathing was deep and even.

Suddenly Sooshewan was aware of voices sounding far away. She left the shelter, wondering if she were dreaming. But the voices were there, down by the shore. And they were calling her name. Sooshewan ran and threw herself on her stomach, looking over the edge of the cliff.

There stood her uncle and two other men from the village. The boy who had killed the ptarmigan was with them.

"Uncle," she called. "I'm up here."

Sooshewan told her story while her uncle looked at her father's injuries and the others built a larger shelter. Then she lay down and slept peacefully in the little shelter.

Much later, Sooshewan woke. Slowly she became aware of two sensations which brought her great comfort: the strong smell of boiling seal meat and the sound of her father's voice.

One of the men had killed a seal and everyone was feasting. Sooshewan was greeted with happy grins when she poked her head out of the shelter.

"Come and eat, little brave one," her uncle said. "There is plenty for us and more to take back to the village."

"Where is my father?" asked Sooshewan.

"We moved him to the new shelter," said her uncle.

Sooshewan found her father awake but very weak.

"Your uncle has told me what you did, Sooshewan," he whispered. "You have saved my life."

"Oh, but it was Grandmother," said Sooshewan. "She told me what to do."

Just then, the boy came to the shelter. "Come, Woas-sut," he said. "Eat while the meat is hot."

"Yes," said her father. "Go and eat. You deserve a good meal, and you deserve the name *woas-sut.*"

Sooshewan had not realized that the boy had called her woas-sut, woman, and it was strange to hear her father say it.

She and her father hugged one another as they had when she was a baby. Then Sooshewan, woas-sut, proudly joined the others at the meal.